D1142407

The Swan Princess

Based on the story by
Hans Christian Andersen

Retold by Rosie Dickins

Illustrated by Jenny Press

Reading Consultant: Alison Kelly
Roehampton University

Contents

Chapter 1

A royal wedding

Far away and long ago, there was
a land where the swallows flew to
spend the winter. The King of that
land had eleven sons and one
daughter – Eliza.

The Queen had died when Eliza
was born, but her father and
brothers looked after her. Her
father was kind and her brothers
were handsome and noble...

...most of the time. Eliza spent
hours playing with them.

While the princes were at school,
Eliza sat and looked at beautiful
picture books, or watched swallows
swoop past. She couldn't have been
happier.

One bitterly cold winter, the King married again. His new wife was tall and elegant, and everyone admired her.

She's so beautiful...

But she had a dark secret. The new Queen was a witch!

The King and Queen celebrated
their wedding with a feast. As they
sat down to eat, there was a
croaking under the table and three
warty toads hopped out.

"These are my pets," said the
Queen. "My little toadie-woadies."

Suddenly, there was a loud *ping* and one of the toads leaped into the air. Prince Jasper peeked from behind a chair with a big grin.

"Jasper, I've told you not to use your catapult indoors," the King scolded.

I will teach that boy a lesson!

Before the King could say any more, the servants brought in an enormous wedding cake. Everyone was given a slice – except Eliza and her brothers.

The Queen passed them bowls full of sand. "You can pretend it's cake," she told them.

"I'm not eating that!" retorted Prince Julian.

"Julian, behave yourself. Eat up!" snapped the King, who couldn't see the sand.

Boys can be so difficult...

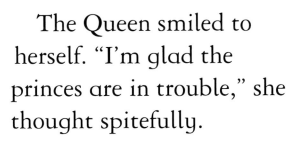

The Queen smiled to herself. "I'm glad the princes are in trouble," she thought spitefully.

Chapter 2

Wild swans

> I shall cast a spell on the princes.

The new Queen hated children.
First, she hatched a plan to get rid
of her stepsons.

A week later, the princes came home from school to find the Queen barring their way to the castle.

"You're not wanted here. Go and fend for yourselves," she shouted. "Fly away like wild birds!"

The horrified princes began to
sprout white feathers. As they tried
to speak, their mouths turned into
beaks. Then, instead of eleven
princes, there were eleven swans,
flying out to sea.

13

The Queen went inside and told
the King the princes had run away.

They're wicked,
ungrateful boys.

Now there was just Eliza...

The Queen didn't dare cast another spell, in case the King became suspicious. So she persuaded the King to send Eliza away to live on a farm.

"The fresh air will do Eliza good," she told him.

Eliza went to live with a poor
farmer and his wife, far away from
the palace. She missed her books
and the swallows. But she missed
her father and brothers most of all.

When Eliza was sixteen, the King summoned her back to the castle. Now she was grown up, he wanted her to take her place at the court.

The Queen was waiting for her. She was very jealous when she saw how beautiful Eliza had become. "I'll soon change that," she thought.

"You must be tired," she said to Eliza. "Why don't you have a bath?"

When Eliza wasn't looking, the Queen picked up her toads. One by one, she dropped them into the bath and cast a spell.

The first toad would make Eliza ugly...

...the second toad would make her stupid...

...and the third would make her wicked.

18

But Eliza was too good to be
enchanted by such an evil spell.
When she stepped
into the bath, the
toads turned into
flowers. Their red
petals floated
gently on
the water.

Hmm... I need
a new plan.

When Eliza finished washing, the Queen offered to help again. She made Eliza sit down away from the mirror. Then she wiped Eliza's face with walnut juice, and tangled her hair while pretending to comb it.

Your hair is so pretty.

Now, Eliza looked nothing like
her beautiful self. When she went
to greet her father, he didn't even
recognize her.

"Who let this wild creature in?"
he shouted. "Take it away!"

The guards tried to seize her.

Eliza slipped
between them and ran
out of the castle, sobbing.

Chapter 3

In the forest

In despair, Eliza ran into the forest to hide. She wandered around for hours, until she grew very thirsty. Finding a lake at the edge of the forest, she knelt down to drink...

...and gasped in horror at the face she saw in the water.

The face gasped too. It was her own reflection.

The Queen did this to me.

Eliza quickly washed her face and combed her hair with her fingers. When she had finished, she looked like herself again.

By now, the sun was beginning
to set. Eliza shivered and looked
around to see where she might
spend the night.

Something in the distance caught
her eye. A group of swans was
flying over the trees.

The swans flew closer and closer.
As the sun sank into the west, they
landed on the lake.

25

They shook their wings and, to Eliza's astonishment…

…suddenly, instead of swans, her brothers stood before her.

Eliza was overjoyed. When they had all finished hugging, Prince Julian told her what had happened.

26

"The Queen's spell turned us into
swans," he explained, "but we
become human again at night. We
can visit our old home only once a
year. Tomorrow, we must fly away."

"If you're going, I'm coming too,"
Eliza decided.

Eliza and her brothers spent all night weaving a net of rushes, so the swans would be able to carry her when they flew.

It was nearly dawn by the time they finished. Eliza was so tired, she just lay down where she was and fell asleep.

Chapter 4

Eliza's dream

When Eliza woke, she felt wind
rushing past and opened her eyes.
She was in the net, surrounded by
flapping wings. Below, there was
nothing but water. She realized
they were over the sea.

Beside her was a branch of
berries Jasper had picked. So Eliza
had berries for breakfast – and for
lunch and supper too.

They spent all day flying. Clouds
blew by and waves bobbed below.
At last, as the sun began to sink,
she saw a smudge of land on the
horizon.

As dusk fell, they landed. Once again, the swans shed their feathers.

"This is our home now," Julian told Eliza, showing her a cave carpeted with soft, green moss.

That night, Eliza dreamed she was still flying through the clouds.

In the dream, one of the clouds took on the shape of a castle. A beautiful fairy came out of the castle and spoke to her.

"Eliza," the fairy said. "If you are brave, you can save your brothers from the Queen's spell."

"How?" pleaded Eliza.

"By making each one a shirt of nettles," the fairy replied. "When they put on the shirts, the spell will be broken."

"But you must make the shirts in silence," the fairy warned. "If you speak even a word before the spell is ended, your brothers will die."

Eliza reached out to touch a nettle. It stung her fingers – and she woke with a start.

"It was only a dream," thought Eliza. "But what if it's true? I have to try..."

Her brothers were still asleep as she tiptoed out. Nettles seemed to grow everywhere in this strange new land. Bravely, she picked a huge armful. They stung her hands, but she didn't make a sound.

When she got back to the cave, it was broad daylight and her brothers had flown away. She set to work at once, stripping the nettle stems and weaving them together.

By evening, her fingers were covered in blisters, but Eliza didn't mind. She had almost finished the first shirt.

The princes returned at sunset. They understood at once what Eliza was trying to do. They thanked her, but she could not reply.

Prince Jasper wept to see her sore fingers. Where his tears touched her skin, it healed at once.

Chapter 5

Another wedding

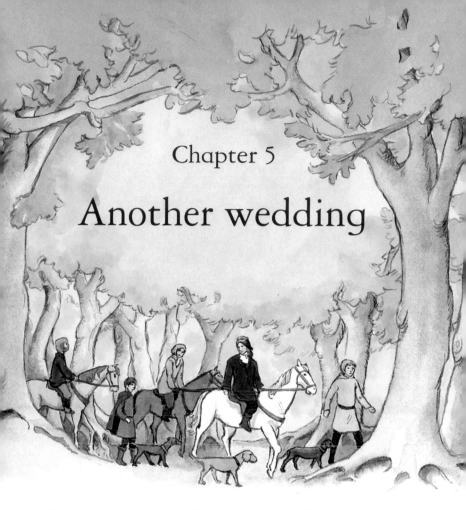

The next day, Eliza set off to pick more nettles. The same day, the King of the land decided to go hunting. He was riding through the woods when he saw Eliza.

The King was struck by Eliza's beauty. "What is your name?" he asked. But Eliza only shook her head and went on picking nettles.

"Why are you picking nettles?" the King demanded. But Eliza did not reply.

"She can't talk," the King decided. "Let's take her back to the palace, so we can look after her."

Eliza shook her head – but it was no good. A strong huntsman picked her up and placed her on his horse.

When they reached the palace, the King showed Eliza around. She gazed sadly at the marble floors and painted ceilings.

When they came to the garden, she looked around hopefully. But there were no nettles anywhere – only fountains and rose bushes and smooth, green grass.

Then, in the distance, she saw an old church. It looked very rundown. On one side was a row of crumbling tombstones, overgrown with nettles.

I'm sorry it's such a mess.

"We don't use this place much since we built the cathedral," the King explained.

Eliza just smiled. "I can still make the shirts," she thought with relief.

41

Before long, the King was in love with the beautiful girl from the woods. He didn't seem to mind her silence.

When Eliza spent all day weaving nettles, he gave her soft gloves to cover her blistered fingers. And his kindness made Eliza love him in return.

Soon the King had made up his mind. He went to find Eliza, who was sitting beside a heap of nettles.

"Will you marry me?" he asked.

Eliza could not answer in words, but she smiled and nodded – and continued weaving nettles.

"Um... good," said the King. "Well, I'd better go and see about the wedding."

I hope she's not going to weave nettles forever!

The King summoned his Archbishop. "I'm getting married," the King told him.

The Archbishop threw up his hands in horror. He thought Eliza was a witch and the King was under her spell. "Your majesty," he pleaded, "you hardly know the girl. And what is she doing with all those nettles?"

I'm sure she's up to no good!

"I don't care," said the King stubbornly. "I'll marry her anyway!" And he stomped off to the kitchens to give orders for a royal feast.

I want a huge cake and a hundred kinds of ice cream...

Meanwhile, Eliza continued weaving. By the night before the wedding, she had made ten shirts. "I'll finish the last one tonight," she thought happily.

As she started on the final shirt, she realized she would need more nettles. "Well, I'll just have to go out and pick some," she decided.

Outside, it was so dark she could barely see the graveyard. She shivered. "There's no such thing as ghouls or ghosts!" she told herself bravely.

The Archbishop
was still awake,
worrying about
the wedding.

He saw Eliza slip out and
decided to follow her. "Only a
witch would pick nettles at
midnight," he told himself.

When Eliza began wandering among the tombstones, he decided he had seen enough.

"Stop, witch!" he cried.

His shout brought the palace guards running. On his orders, they seized Eliza and threw her into prison.

49

Chapter 6

Nettle shirts

The next day, instead of a wedding, there was a trial. Eliza was brought before the judge in chains.

The Archbishop stood up.
"I saw her picking nettles in the
graveyard at midnight," he cried.
"She must be a witch!"

"Well, what do you say to that?"
the judge asked Eliza.
But she just shook
her head sadly.
She could not
speak to defend
herself.

Then the King tried to speak for
her. "She's innocent!" he insisted.

But the Archbishop had an
answer for that. "She has bewitched
the King," he told the court. "He
doesn't know what he is saying."

The judge frowned. "I agree with the Archbishop," he said. "The girl is a witch. She will be executed tomorrow."

The King was heartbroken, but the judge had made up his mind. There was nothing the King could do.

Eliza was taken back to prison and locked in a tiny cell. "I'd nearly finished the coats," she thought desperately, "but now I'll never see my brothers again!" She felt completely miserable.

Suddenly, something fluttered against the window and a white swan feather drifted down.

Eliza looked up – and saw Jasper looking back. Her brothers had been searching for her ever since she disappeared. She smiled, in spite of everything.

The door burst open and the jailer looked in. "You'll need some covers for tonight," he sneered. "The King asked me to give you these. I hope you find them comfortable."

A bundle landed at Eliza's feet, and the door slammed shut.

Eliza opened the bundle. Something green and bristly fell out. It was the nettle shirts.

55

"I mustn't give up," Eliza told herself. She held up the shirts so Jasper could see them. He bowed his head and then flew away. "Perhaps he's gone to fetch the others," she thought.

The last shirt was still a pile of
unwoven stems. Quickly, Eliza
set to work again.

She wove all night. By dawn, she
had made the body and one sleeve.
And then she ran out
of nettles.

Oh no!

There wasn't even a stem left for the last sleeve. "It'll just have to do," Eliza decided, gathering the shirts together. "I hope it works."

Minutes later, there was a bang on the door. The guards had come to take her away. They led her outside, still clutching the shirts.

A huge crowd had gathered to
see the execution. Before it could
start, there was a startled murmur
and people began pointing at the
sky. Eleven white swans were
flying closer and closer.

59

The swans swooped down. One by one, they swept past Eliza, so she could throw the shirts over them. The crowd gasped.

There was a shimmering in the air and then, instead of the swans, there were eleven young men standing beside Eliza.

At the same time, Eliza's chains
turned into white roses and fell to
the ground. The spell was finally
broken – and Eliza could speak.

"Oh Jasper," cried Eliza, "you've still got a swan's wing!"

"I don't mind," he replied, giving her a big, feathery hug.

I'm not a witch!

Then the King spoke. "I don't know what's going on here," he said, "but perhaps you can tell me at the wedding feast..."

"...if you still want to marry me?"
he continued, turning shyly to Eliza.

"Oh yes!" said Eliza, smiling.

"And at this wedding," Jasper put
in, with a grin, "I'm going to make
sure I get a real slice of cake!"

The Swan Princess has been told many times in many countries. This retelling is based on a version by Hans Christian Andersen. He called his story *The Wild Swans*.

Hans Christian Andersen was born in Denmark in 1805, the son of a poor shoemaker. He left home at fourteen to seek his fortune and became famous all over the world as a writer of fairy tales.

Series editor: Lesley Sims
Cover design by Russell Punter

First published in 2005 by Usborne Publishing Ltd., Usborne House, 83-85 Saffron Hill, London EC1N 8RT, England. www.usborne.com
Copyright © 2005 Usborne Publishing Ltd.

All rights reserved. No part of this publication may be reproduced, stored in a retrieval system or transmitted in any form or by any means, electronic, mechanical, photocopying, recording or otherwise without the prior permission of the publisher. The name Usborne and the devices ♀ ⊕ are Trade Marks of Usborne Publishing Ltd. Printed in China. UE. First published in America in 2005.